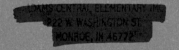

PICK, PULL, SNAP!

Where Once a Flower Bloomed

BY Lola M. Schaefer

ILLUSTRATED BY Lindsay Barrett George

Greenwillow Books
An Imprint of HarperCollinsPublishers

Pick, Pull, Snap!: Where Once a Flower Bloomed. Text copyright © 2003 by Lola M. Schaefer. Illustrations copyright © 2003 by Lindsay Barrett George.
Manufactured in China. www.harperchildrens.com Gouache paints were used to prepare the full-color art. The text type is Cochin.
Library of Congress Cataloging-in-Publication Data: Schaefer, Lola M., (date). Pick, pull, snap! : where once a flower bloomed / by Lola M. Schaefer ; pictures by Lindsay Barrett George.
   p.   cm. "Greenwillow Books." Summary: Describes how raspberries, peanuts, corn, and other foods are produced as various plants flower, create seeds, and finally bear fruit. ISBN 0-688-17834-0
1. Plants—Reproduction—Juvenile literature. 2. Flowers—Juvenile literature. 3. Fruit—Juvenile literature. 4. Seeds—Juvenile literature. [1. Plants. 2. Flowers. 3. Fruit. 4. Seeds.]   I. George, Lindsay
Barrett, ill.   II. Title.   QK825.S34 2003   571.8'2—dc21   2002066818   First Edition   10 9 8 7 6 5 4

Greenwillow Books

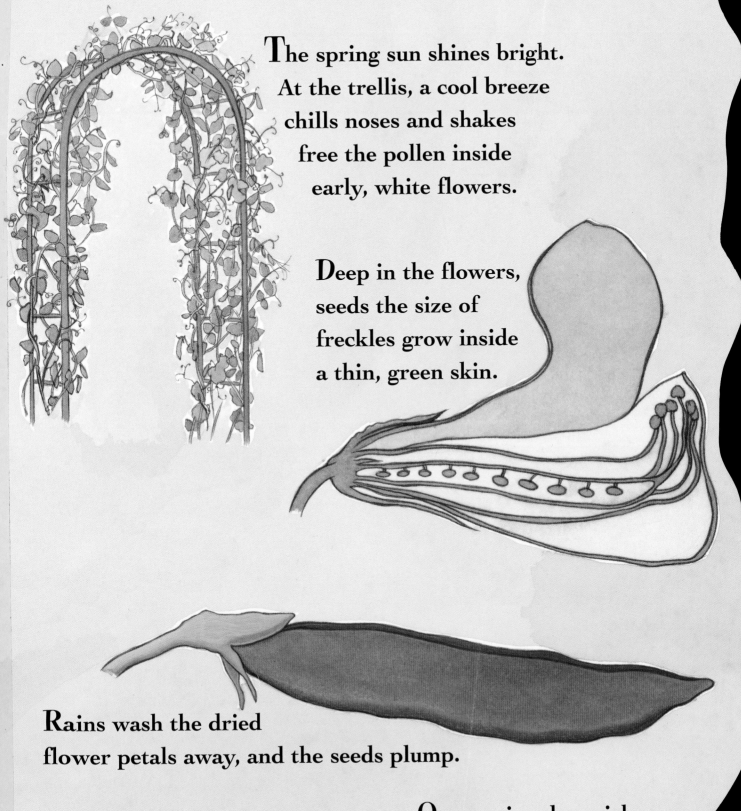

The spring sun shines bright. At the trellis, a cool breeze chills noses and shakes free the pollen inside early, white flowers.

Deep in the flowers, seeds the size of freckles grow inside a thin, green skin.

Rains wash the dried flower petals away, and the seeds plump.

On a spring day, pick . . .

handfuls of pea pods
from the vines
where once a flower bloomed.

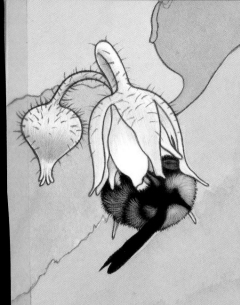

In the berry patch,
bumblebees zigzag
from blossom to blossom,
spreading pollen inside
delicate white flowers
no bigger than a fingertip.

Deep inside
the flowers,
hard seeds grow
in bits of fruit
that form a cluster.

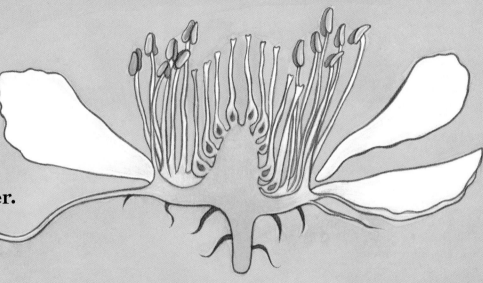

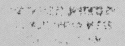

The flowers curl
and blow away,
and in a few weeks
the fruit turns red
in the warm sunshine.

On a summer morning, pull . . .

ripe raspberries from the bush
where once a flower bloomed.

For Molly, who enjoys the gardening
as much as the harvest
—L. S.

For Susie, a very special gardener
—L. B. G.

Special thanks to Dr. Orzolek, Dr. Ferretti, Dr. Mozingo,
Dave Nonnemacher, Susann George, Jody Taylor,
and especially Zachary Melling, Jessica LeBlanc,
Matt Nonnemacher, and Cammy George
—L. B. G.

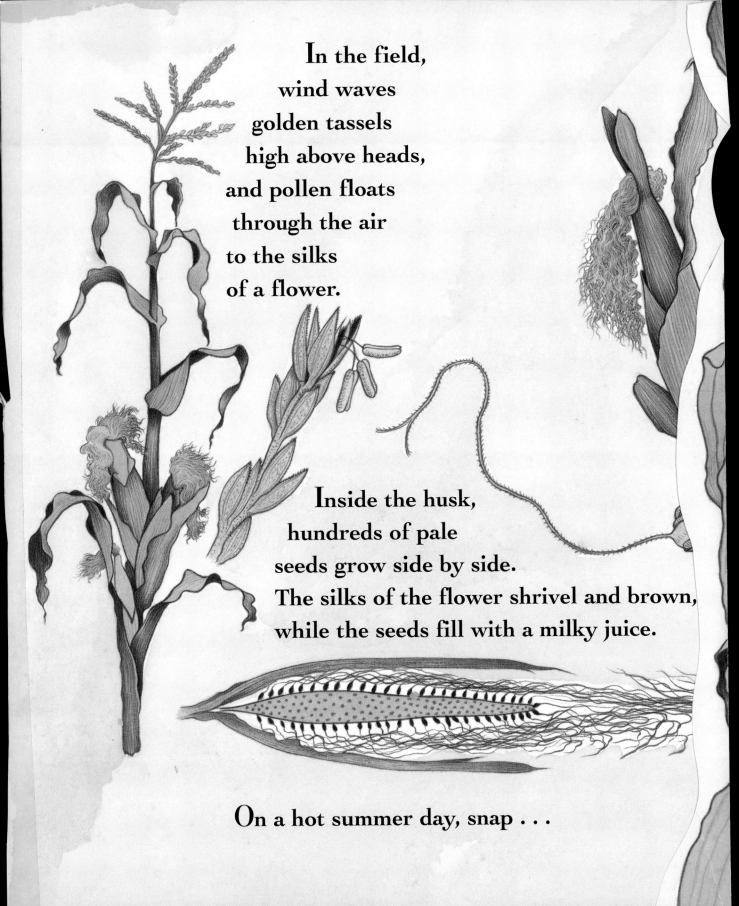

In the field,
wind waves
golden tassels
high above heads,
and pollen floats
through the air
to the silks
of a flower.

Inside the husk,
hundreds of pale
seeds grow side by side.
The silks of the flower shrivel and brown,
while the seeds fill with a milky juice.

On a hot summer day, snap . . .

an ear of corn from the stalk
where once a flower bloomed.

a fuzzy peach from the tree
where once a flower bloomed.

In the orchard,
a honeybee buzzes
from tree to tree,
flying in and out
of blossoms.

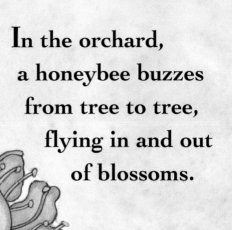

Its legs brush pollen
inside a fragrant,
pink flower.

Deep inside the flower,
a small, green fruit
grows around one seed.

The petals fade
and drop to the ground.

Weeks pass, and the fruit,
large and sweet, hangs
low near passing eyes.

On a late summer day, twist . . .

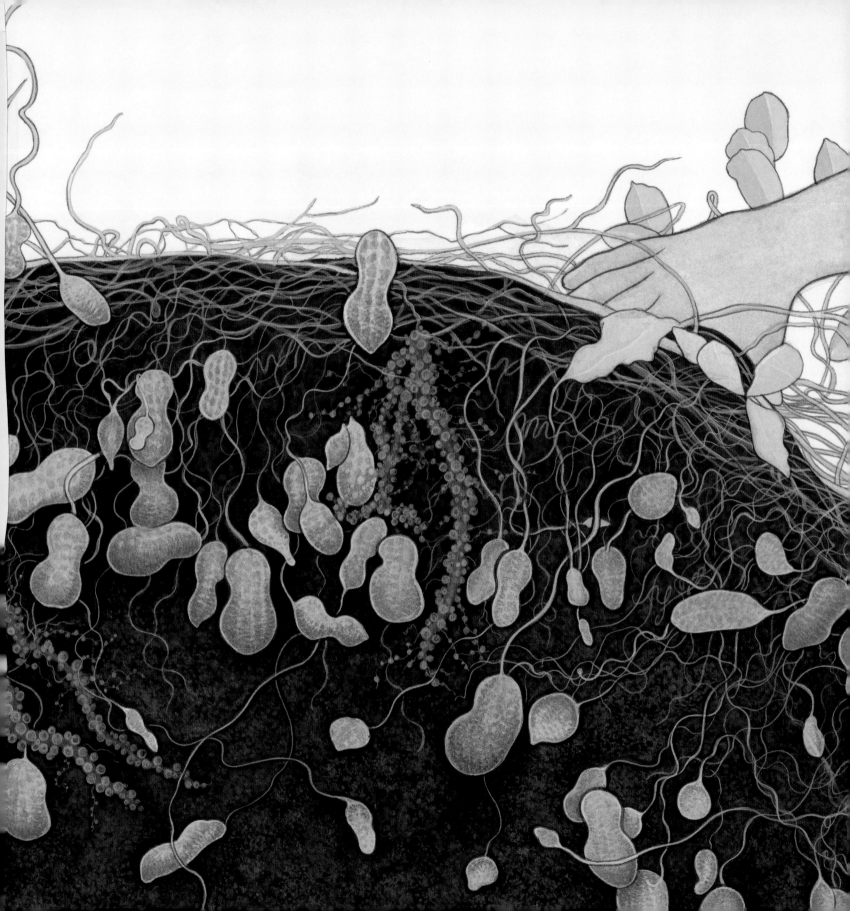

hidden peanuts from under the bush
where once a flower bloomed.

On a sandy hill,
yellow blossoms open
on knee-high plants,
spilling soft pollen
between their petals.
At evening, they close
and wilt.

From the blossoms,
pegs grow and
push into the soil.
Underground, the tips of the pegs
become stiff shells, each holding
two seeds wrapped in red skins.

On a hot
summer day, pull . . .

Now winter winds blow past
the empty trellis,
spindly canes,
bleached stalks,
bare trees,
withered plants,
and wrinkled vines.
But in the spring, plants blossom again.
Pollen dusts the inside of flowers,
and seeds and fruit begin to grow.
On a bright warm day,
gather a new harvest
where once a flower bloomed.

Winter

JANUARY

FEBRUARY

MARCH

Spring

APRIL

MAY

JUNE

Summer

JULY

AUGUST

SEPTEMBER

OCTOBER

NOVEMBER

DECEMBER

Fall

From Flower to Fruit

Every seed or fruit begins in a flower. A bee enters a flower, looking for a food called nectar. Soft hairs on its legs and body pick up grains of pollen. Then the bee flies to another flower and carries the pollen with it. Some of the pollen falls off the bee's body and into the second flower. This is called pollination. Deep inside the flower, the pollen reaches a part of the plant called the pistil. This is called fertilization. After a flower is fertilized, seeds and fruit begin to grow.

anther

petal

stamen

pistil

Bees are just one type of pollinator. Beetles, flies, ants, butterflies, hummingbirds, and bats can be pollinators, too. Sometimes pollen is carried from flower to flower by wind or water. Other flowers, like the tomato and the peanut, pollinate themselves. In those plants, a flower's pollen ripens and falls onto its own pistil, and a seed begins to grow.

PEAS
Plant peas in early spring, in full sun. Sow the seeds about 1 inch deep, and place them in rows about 2 inches apart from each other. Plant climbing peas next to a trellis. Weed your peas and keep the soil moist. Pick fresh peas in 60 to 70 days (about 2 months).

PEA

RASPBERRY BUSHES
Plant raspberry bushes in loose soil in the spring. In a sunny spot, dig a hole large enough for the roots. Cover the roots with 1 inch of soil. Plant bushes 2 feet apart. Weed between your bushes, and be patient. Your first raspberries will be ready to pick in 2 years.

**a heavy orange pumpkin
from the vine
where once a flower bloomed.**

CORN

Plant corn in warm, well-drained soil in the spring. Corn grows best in full sun. Make small hills about 3 feet wide and sow 6 seeds in each hill. When the corn sprouts, keep 3 plants in each hill and pull up the rest. You can also sow corn in rows; the rows should be 30 inches apart. When the corn sprouts, leave 1 plant every 8 to 12 inches and pull up the rest. Weed regularly. Pick ears of ripe corn in 70 to 80 days (2 to 3 months).

PEACH TREE

To grow your own peach tree, plant a clean, dry peach stone in a pot of rich dirt. Push the stone into the soil to a depth of 3 to 4 times its height. Keep the soil moist. After the plant sprouts, keep it on a sunny windowsill until spring.

Plant peach trees on a sunny, well-drained slope in early spring. Dig a hole twice the size of the roots. Fill the bottom half of the hole with rich soil. Spread the roots over the soil and hold the tree straight. Cover the roots with soil, water, then add more soil until the hole is filled. Plant trees 20 feet apart. Peaches will grow in 3 to 4 years.

PEANUTS

Plant peanuts in full sun after the last frost in spring. They grow best in warm, loose, well-drained soil. Sow seeds 2 to 3 inches deep. Grow plants 6 inches apart in raised beds or in rows that are 30 inches apart. You can dig or pull peanuts in 120 to 140 days (between 4 and 5 months) or when leaves are yellow. Dry peanuts in the sun before shelling or roasting.

PUMPKINS

Plant pumpkin seeds in loose soil in spring after the ground is warm. Make small hills 20 to 30 inches across. The hills need to be 6 to 8 feet apart and in full sun. Sow 4 to 6 seeds in each hill. Seeds can also be planted in rows. After the pumpkins sprout, leave one plant every 2 or 3 feet and pull up the rest. Mulch between plants with straw or plastic. Pick ripe pumpkins in 110 to 120 days (3 to 4 months).

Glossary

anther: the part of a plant at the end of the stamen. It holds pollen.

blossom: a flower

bumblebee: a large bee with bright yellow and black stripes

fertilization: in plants, the process of combining pollen with the pistil. After fertilization, seeds and fruit can grow.

flower: the part of the plant that produces seeds, fruit, or both. Flowers are usually brightly colored.

fruit: the part of the plant that holds the seeds

honeybee: a small bee that collects nectar and uses it to make honey in a hive. Honeybees collect pollen to feed to their young.

husk: the outer covering of leaves that surrounds and protects an ear of corn

mulch: a layer of straw, plastic, grass, or compost spread between plants to prevent erosion, evaporation, or the growth of weeds

nectar: a sweet liquid found in many plant flowers. Nectar is food for many insects, birds, and bats.

peg: a stem that grows from the flower of a peanut plant

petal: one of the outer sections of the flower

pistil: the part of the flower that produces seeds

pollen: tiny yellow grains produced by the stamen of a plant

pollination: the process of transferring pollen from the anthers to the pistil of a flower

pollinator: something that transfers pollen from the anthers to the pistil of a flower. Common pollinators are insects, birds, bats, wind, and water.

seed: the fertilized part of the flowering plant from which a new plant can grow

self-pollination: the process of transferring pollen from the anthers to the pistil of the same flower. Self-pollination occurs when the pollen ripens and falls from the anther to the pistil.

silk: a long, thin fiber that is attached to a kernel, or seed, of corn and extends out of the husk. Pollen falls on the silk and grows through it to reach the corn kernel for fertilization.

sow: to plant or scatter seeds to grow

stalk: the long main stem of a plant, from which the leaves and flowers grow. Corn stalks can grow more than ten feet tall.

stamen: the part of a flower that makes pollen

trellis: a framework of wood, wire, or plastic that supports a growing plant

In the garden,
a bumblebee darts
between giant blossoms,
entering one
after another,
scattering pollen
inside a yellow
flower opened wide.

er the flower, flat, smooth seeds grow
round, hard fruit. The petals droop,
each day the fruit grows bigger
bigger and bigger.

e last day
f summer, roll . . .